Mommy, Where Are You?

Harriet Ziefert

Emilie Boon

Puffin Books

PUFFIN BOOKS
Published by the Penguin Group
Viking Penguin Inc., 40 West 23rd Street, New York, New York 10010, U.S.A.
Penguin Books Ltd, 27 Wrights Lane, London W8 5TZ England
Penguin Books Australia Ltd, Ringwood, Victoria, Australia
Penguin Books Canada Ltd, 2801 John Street, Markham, Ontario, Canada L3R 1B4
Penguin Books (N.Z.) Ltd, 182–190 Wairau Road, Auckland 10, New Zealand

Penguin Books Ltd, Registered Offices: Harmondsworth, Middlesex, England

First published in Picture Puffins, 1988

Published simultaneously in Canada

Text copyright © Harriet Ziefert, 1988

Illustrations copyright © Emilie Boon, 1988

Printed in Singapore for Harriet Ziefert, Inc.

Library of Congress catalog number: 87-63281

ISBN 0-14-050894-5

I'm looking
for my mommy.

Mommy,
is that you?

Mommy,
I can't see you!

Mommy,
where are you?

Mommy, what are you doing?

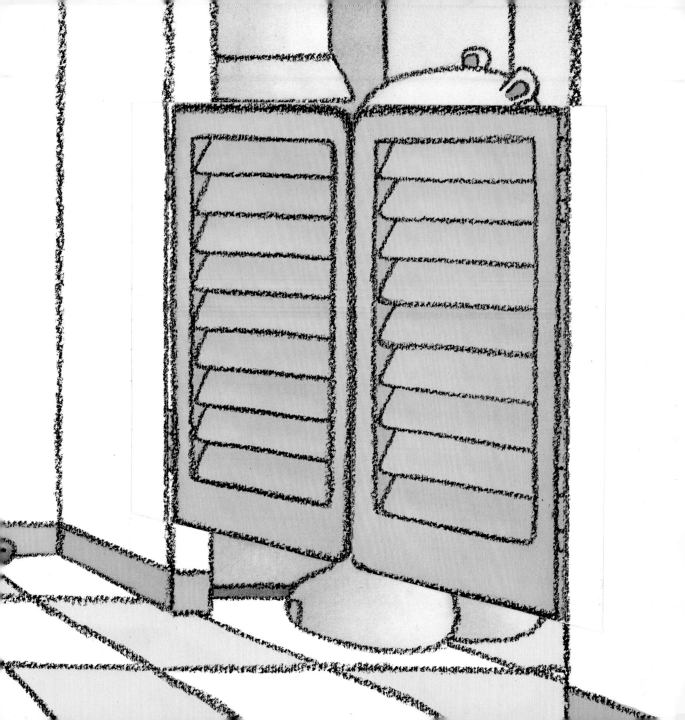

Mommy,
where are you?

Little Hippo,
where are you?

Good night, Mommy!